Przemysław Wechterowicz   Emilia Dziubak

HUG ME, PLEASE!

First published in the United States in 2017 by
words & pictures, Part of The Quarto Group,
6 Orchard, Lake Forest, CA 92630

A CIP record for the book is available from the Library of Congress.

ISBN: 978-1-68297-142-0

1 3 5 7 9 8 6 4 2

Printed in China

Przemysław Wechterowicz   Emilia Dziubak

HUG ME, PLEASE!

words & pictures

One morning, as the Sun was still brushing its teeth,
Little Bear and Daddy Bear went for a stroll.
"What shall we do today, Daddy?" Little Bear asked.
"Let's look for some honey!" Daddy Bear replied.

The honey was delicious. It gave them a warm, sweet feeling inside. "I know what we could do now," Little Bear said. "Visit Mr. Beaver and give him a big hug!"

"A brilliant idea, son!" said Daddy Bear. "It's sure to brighten up his day."
And off they went. Along the way, they chatted about how lucky they were to have one another. And before they knew it, they had reached Mr. Beaver's.

Mr. Beaver was working so hard that Little Bear
and Daddy Bear danced to get his attention.
"Hello! We have come to hug you!" said Daddy Bear.
Mr. Beaver was frightened. "Why?" he asked.
"To brighten up your day," said Little Bear.
So Mr. Beaver agreed to a little hug. It felt
strange but nice.

"Dad, do you think Mr. Beaver liked his hug?"
Little Bear asked.

"I think so," Daddy Bear replied. "Hugging always
makes you feel good."

They were heading home when Little Bear pulled his
dad's fur. "Can we hug someone else now?" he asked.

"Of course! Hugging is a fine way to spend your day!"
Daddy Bear smiled.

Miss Weasel was reading when she heard Little Bear.

"Excuse me, can we have a hug, please?"

Miss Weasel jumped. "You almost scared me to death!"

Little Bear apologized, then hugged Miss Weasel in the most calming way he knew how.

Next they met two hares eating fresh carrots.

"Ahem," Daddy Bear said. "May we try some of those?"

The hares froze. Not their precious carrots!

Daddy Bear nibbled one carrot. Little Bear nibbled another.

"I don't like these carrots much," said Daddy Bear.

"I don't either," said Little Bear. "I prefer hugs."

The hares were relieved. "If you'd prefer a hug

instead of a carrot, we'd be happy to help."

The Big Bad Wolf was sharpening his claws.

"Have you seen a girl in a red hood?" he asked.

Daddy Bear shook his head.

Little Bear smiled. "We would like to give you a hug," he said.

The wolf looked at them suspiciously. "All right. But not too hard!"

The wolf enjoyed the hug so much that he didn't notice

a little girl in a red hood skipping past.

By the stream, Old Mr. Elk was having a drink.

"Would you mind if we gave you a hug?" Little Bear asked.

"But why hug an old beast like me?" Old Mr. Elk said.

"Because it will make you feel good."

Old Mr. Elk had to admit, Little Bear's hug *was* perfect.

In a clearing, a stranger was basking in the Sun.

"I didn't know that anacondas lived in our forest," said Daddy Bear.

Ms. Anaconda hissed gently. "I'm visiting Grass Snake. What are you doing?"

"We're hugging everyone we meet," Little Bear piped up. "Would you like us to hug you?"

Ms. Anaconda smiled. "It would be my pleasure."

Next they passed through a
meadow of sweet-smelling flowers,
and Little Bear shouted, "Look at that
colorful caterpillar! It's like a rainbow!"
Mrs. Caterpillar sat up. "Out of my way!
I want to snuggle up in my cocoon."
"Could I give you one little hug
before you go to sleep?"
"Be quick!" said
Mrs. Caterpillar.
So Little Bear hugged her
as quickly, and as delicately,
as he could.

Behind a bush, the bears spied a hunter.

Little Bear whispered: "Do you think we can hug him?"

"It would be rude not to," Daddy Bear replied.

So they picked up the hunter and hugged him hard.

"I will look after his net," said Daddy Bear.

On their way home, they hugged more animals.

"Hello, Mr. Badger."

"This is cozy!"

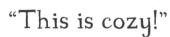

"Ooh la la! What big muscles!"

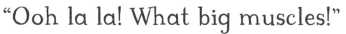

"One at a time, children!"

"What a great guy!"

"Wait for us!"

It was turning out to be one of the best days of Little Bear's life.

They were almost home when suddenly Little Bear sat down.

"Dad, haven't we forgotten someone?"

Daddy Bear stopped. He counted everyone who lived in the forest.

"I'm pretty sure we've hugged everyone."

"But Dad—think!"

Daddy Bear counted again. "I give up, son. Who have we missed?"

"Each other, Daddy!"

And they gave each other the strongest, hardest, longest, largest, and most loving hug of all.

The End